I0668780

Anonymous

Message of His Excellency Joseph E. Brown

to the extra session of the legislature, convened March 10th, 1864. Vol. 2

Anonymous

Message of His Excellency Joseph E. Brown
to the extra session of the legislature, convened March 10th, 1864. Vol. 2

ISBN/EAN: 9783337428358

Printed in Europe, USA, Canada, Australia, Japan

Cover: Foto ©Andreas Hilbeck / pixelio.de

More available books at **www.hansebooks.com**

MESSAGE

OF

HIS EXCELLENCY JOSEPH E. BROWN,

TO THE

EXTRA SESSION OF THE LEGISLATURE,

CONVENED MARCH 10TH, 1864,

Upon the Currency Act; Secret sessions of Congress; The late Conscription Act; The un-
constitutionality of the Act suspending
the privilege of the Writ of Habeas
Corpus, in cases of illegal arrests made by the President;
The causes of the War and manner of conduct-
ing it; And the terms upon which
peace should be sought, &c.

BOUGHTON, NISBET, BARNES & MOORE, State Printer
MILLEDGEVILLE, GA.,
::::::::::::::::::
1864.

MESSAGE.

EXECUTIVE DEPARTMENT, } .
MILLEDGEVILLE, GA., March 10th 1864. }

To the Senate and House of Representatives :

The patriotic zeal exhibited by you at your late session, for the promotion of the interest and protection of the liberties of the country, and the personal kindness and official courtesy which I received at your hands, and for which I renew my thanks, have satisfied me that laying aside all past party names, issues and strifes, your object as legislators is to discharge faithfully your official duties, and to sacrifice all private interests and personal preferences to the public good. In view of these considerations, I feel that I can rely upon your counsels as a tower of strength in time of darkness and gloom. I have therefore convened you that I may have the benefit of your advice and assistance, at this critical juncture in our State and Confederate affairs.

TRANSPORTATION OF CORN TO INDIGENT SOLDIERS FAMILIES.

Since your adjournment, experience has shown that it is not possible without assistance from the State, which will require further legislation, for the agents of the counties, where there is great scarcity of provisions, to secure transportation for the corn purchased in South Western and Middle Georgia, to the places where it is needed. To meet this difficulty, I respectfully recommend the passage of a law, authorizing the Quarter-Master General of this State, or such other officer as the Governor may from time to time designate, under the order of the Governor, to take possession of and control any of the Rail Roads in the State, with their rolling stock, or any other available conveyance, and require that corn or other provisions for the needy or for the county agents for soldiers families, be transported in preference to all other articles or things, except the troops and the supplies necessary for the support of the armies of the Confederate States, and that the act provide for the payment of just compensation, for the use of such means of transportation, while in possession of the authorized officers of this State—the compensation to be paid out of the money already appropriated as a relief fund, by the agents or persons at whose request the transportation may be furnished.

Experience has also proved, that the counties of North Eastern Georgia most remote from the Railroad, cannot obtain sufficient means of transportation to carry the corn from the Rail Road to the place of consumption. The scarcity of teams is owing to the fact that their horses have been taken for cavalry service, and their oxen have been impressed for beef for the army. Finding that there was likely to be much suffering in that section for bread for soldiers' families, I ordered the energetic Quarter Master General of the State, to purchase teams and wagons, by drafts upon the military fund, and aid those most destitute and most remote from the Rail Road, in the transportation of the corn. If this action is approved by the Legislature, as I trust it will be, the teams now about ready for use, can be employed in this service for a portion of the year. If not approved they will at any time command more in the market than they cost the State, if not needed for military uses.

RELIEF FUND FOR SOLDIERS' FAMILIES.

I am satisfied that the indigent families of soldiers in many of the counties of this State, are not receiving the benefits to which they are entitled, on account of the neglect or mismanagement of the Inferior Courts. Six millions of dollars have been appropriated for this purpose for the present year. which, if properly applied, is sufficient to prevent any actual suffering, Complaints come up constantly that adequate provisions are not made for the needy. In many cases, I have no doubt these complaints are well founded. As evidence of the neglect of part of the Courts, it may be proper to state, that great as the destitution is among those entitled to the fund, the amount due for the last quarter of last year, has not in some cases been applied for. Some Courts have not yet sent in their reports of the number entitled for the present year, so as to enable me to have the calculation made, and the amount due each county ascertained; while many of the counties have made no application for any part of the fund appropriated for this year.

While the Governor has power to require the courts to make reports of the disposition made of the fund, in cases where he suspects it is being improperly applied, and to withhold payments to the courts in such cases; he has no power to compel the courts to do their duty, nor can he take the fund from them and appoint any other person or agent to distribute it among those for whom it is intended. If the courts fail to act, the law makes no other provision for the distribution of the fund. Unless some better plan is adopted, I am satisfied the objects of the Legislature will be very imperfectly carried out in many of the counties, and the needy will not receive the benefits of the liberal provision made for them by the appropriation. As it may be necessary to provide for the appointment of active, reliable agents in the counties, to assist the courts, or to take charge of the fund in case of neglect or mismanagement by them, I respectfully suggest that provision should be made for commissioning all such, as officers of this

State, so as to protect them against conscription. It will be impossible to relieve the needy, if our most valuable county agents are taken from the discharge of their important duties by the enrolling officers of the Confederacy.

Provision should also be made for the removal from office, of all Justices of the Inferior Courts, who neglect or refuse to discharge their duties promptly and faithfully.

COTTON PLANTING.

Having on former occasions, brought the question of farther restriction of cotton planting to the attention of the General Assembly, I feel a delicacy in again recurring to that subject. The present prices of provisions and the great importance of securing a continued supply of the necessaries of life, are my excuse for again earnestly recommending that the law be so changed as to make it highly penal for any person to plant or cultivate, in cotton, more than one quarter of an acre to the hand till the end of the war.

This additional restraint is not necessary to control the conduct of the more liberal and patriotic portion of our people; but there are those, who for the purpose of making a little more money, will plant the last seed allowed by law without stopping to enquire whether they thereby endanger the liberties of the people and the independence of the Confederacy.

To control the conduct of this class of persons, and to the extent of our ability to provide against the possible contingency of a failure of supplies in future, I feel it to be an imperative duty, again to urge upon your consideration the importance of the legislation above recommended.

ILLEGAL DISTILLATION.

I beg leave again to call the attention of the General Assembly to the illegal distillation of grain into spirituous liquors. So great are the profits realized by those engaged in this business, that the law is evaded in every way that ingenuity can devise; and I am satisfied that the evil can not be effectually suppressed without farther and more stringent legislation. Some of the Judges have ruled that the act passed at your last session, does not give them authority to draw and compel the attendance of a jury out of the regular term time of the Court, to try the question of nuisance, while some public officers have shown no disposition to act, for fear of incurring the ill-will of persons of wealth and influence, who are engaged in the daily violation of the law.

Distillers in some parts of the State, are paying ten dollars per bushel for corn to convert into whiskey, while soldiers' families and other poor persons are suffering for bread.

I renew the expression of my firm conviction, that the evil can only be effectually suppressed by the seizure of the stills. We now need copper for the use of the State Road and for military uses, and I earnestly request that an act be passed, authorizing the Governor to impress all the stills in the State which he has reasonable ground to suspect have been used in violation of the law, and convert them into such material for the Road and implements of war, as the State may, need, and that he be authorized to use all the military force necessary to accomplish the object, and that provision be made for paying the owner just compensation for such stills when seized. I also recommend that provision be made for annulling the commission of any civil or military officer of this State, who fails to exercise vigilance, and to discharge his duty faithfully in the execution of the law against illegal distillation.

IMPRESSMENT OF PROVISIONS.

Since your last session, experience has proven that from distrust of the currency or from other cause, many planters have refused to sell corn or other provisions, not necessary for their own use, to State or county agents for the market price when offered, while soldiers' families have been suffering for provisions.

I recommend the enactment of a law authorizing State officers, under the direction of the Governor, to make impressments of provisions in all such cases, and providing for the payment of just compensation to the owners of the property impressed.

SLAVES ESCAPING TO THE ENEMY.

The official reports of Federal officers are said to show that the enemy now has 50,000 of our slaves employed against us. If these 50,000 able bodied negroes had been carried into the interior by their owners, when the enemy approached the locality where they were employed, and put to work clearing land and making provisions, we should to-day have been 50,000 stronger and the enemy that much weaker, making a difference of 100,000 in the present relative strength of the parties to the struggle. When a negro man worth $1,000 upon the gold basis, escapes to the enemy, that sum of the aggregate wealth of the State, upon which she should receive taxes, is lost—one laborer who should be employed in the production of provisions is also lost, while one laborer or one more armed man is added to the strength of the enemy.

It is therefore unjustifiable and unpatriotic for the owner to keep his negroes within such distance of the enemy's lines, as to make it easy for them to escape. This should not be permitted, and to prevent it in future such laws should be enacted as may be necessary to compel their removal by the owner in such case, or to provide for their forfeiture to the State.

. No man has a right to' use his own property so as to
weaken our strength, diminish our provision supply and add
recruits to the army of the enemy.

DESERTION OF OUR CAUSE BY REMOVALS WITHIN THE ENEMY'S.

LINE.

I am informed that a number of persons in the portion of
our State, adjoining to East Tennessee, have lately remov-
ed with their families within the lines of the enemy ; and
carried with them their movable property. Those persons
have never been loyal to the cause of the South ; and they
now avail themselves of the earliest opportunity to unite
with the enemies of their State.

I recommend the enactment of a law, providing for the
confiscation of the property of all such persons; and that
all such property be sold, and the proceeds of the sale applied to the payment of damages done to loyal citizens of
the same section, whose property has been destroyed, by
raids of the enemy, or by armed bands of tories.

I am also informed, that some disloyal persons in'that section,
have deserted from our armies ; or avoiding service have
left their families behind, and gone over to the enemy, and
are now under arms against us. I am happy to learn that
the number of such persons is very small. I recommend the
confiscation of the property of this class of persons also,
and in case they have left families behind, that are a charge
to the county, that no part of the relief fund be allowed
them ; but that they be carried to the enemy's lines, and
turned over to those in whose cause their husbands now
serve.

I also recommend the enactment of such laws as shall
forever disfranchise and *decitizenize* all persons of both classes, should they attempt to return to this State.

THE CURRENCY.

The late action of the Congress of the Confederate States
upon the subject of the currency. has rendered further legislation necessary in this State, upon that question. It can
not be denied that this act has seriously embarrassed the financial system of this State, and has shaken the confidence
of our people in' either the justice of the late Congress or
its competency to manage our financial affairs. Probably
the history of the past furnishes few more striking instances
of unsound policy combined with bad faith.

The Government issues its Treasury notes for $100, and
binds itself, two years after a treaty of peace between the
Confederate States and the United States, to pay the bear-
er that sum, and stipulates upon the face of the note, that
it is fundable in Confederate States stocks or bonds, and
receivable in payment of all public dues, except export duties. The Congress, while the war is still progressing, pas-
ses a statute that this bill shall be funded in about forty

days or one third of it shall be repudiated, and that a tax of ten per cent a month shall be paid for it after that time by the holder, and it shall no longer be receivable in payment of public dues, and if it is not funded by the 1st of January next, the whole debt is repudiated. Did the holder take the note, with any such expectation? ' Was this the contract, and is this the way the government is to keep its faith? If we get rid of the old issues in this way, what guaranty do we give, for better faith, in the · redemption of the next issues? Again, many of the notes have the express promise on their face, that they shall be funded in *eight* per cent bonds. When? The plain import is, and so understood by all at the time of their issue, that it may be done at any time before the day fixed on the face of the note for its payment. With what semblance of good faith then does the government, before that time, compel the holder to receive a *four* per cent bond or lose the whole debt? and what better is this than repudiation? When was it ever before attempted by any government, to compel the funding of almost the entire paper currency of a country, amounting to seven or eight hundred millions of dollars, in forty days? This is certainly a new chapter in financiering.

The country expected the imposition of a heavy tax, and all patriotic citizens were prepared to pay it cheerfully at any reasonable sacrifice; but repudiation and bad faith were not expected, and the authors of it cannot be held guiltless.

The expiring Congress took the precaution to discuss this measure in secret session; so that the individual act of the representative could not reach his constituents, and none could be annoyed during its consideration by the murmurs of public disapprobation being echoed back into the Legislative Hall. And to make assurance doubly sure, they fixed the day for the assembling of their successors, at a time too late to remedy the evil, or afford adequate redress for the wrong.

These *secret sessions* of Congress are becoming a blighting curse to the country. They are used as a convenient mode of covering up from the people, such acts or expressions of their representatives as will not bear investigation in the light of day. Almost every act of usurpation of power, or of bad faith, has been conceived, brought forth and nurtured, in *secret session*. If I mistake not, the British Parliament never discussed a single measure in secret session during the whole period of the Crimean War. But if it is necessary to discuss a few important military measures, such as may relate to the movement of armies, &c., in secret session, it does not follow that discussions of questions pertaining to the currency, the suspension of the writ of *Habeas Corpus*, and the like, should all be conducted in secret session. The people should require all such measures to be discussed with open doors, and the press should have the liberty of reporting and freely criticising the acts of our public servants. In this way the reflection of the popular will back upon the representative, would generally cause the defeat of such unsound measures, as those which are now fastened upon the country in defiance of the will of the people.

But dismissing the past and looking to the future, the inquiry presented for our consideration is, how shall the State authorities act in the management of the finances of the State? . As the Confederate States Treasury notes constitute the currency of the country, the State has been obliged to receive and pay them out, and she must continue to do so. as long as they remain the only circulating medium. The present Legislature has very wisely adopted the policy, in the present depreciated condition of the currency, of collecting by taxation a sufficient sum in currency, to pay the current appropriations of the State Government, instead of adding them to the debt of the State to be paid in future upon the gold basis. If the State issues her own bonds and puts them upon the market, or if she issues her own Treasury notes redeemable at a future day in her bonds, she adds the amount so issued to her permanent indebtedness, and defeats the policy of paying as she goes, as her own bonds or notes would then be out, and could not be redeemed with the Confederate notes when received into her Treasury.

If the State receives in payment of taxes the present Confederate Treasury notes, they will be reduced in amount one-third by act of Congress after 1st April next, and the State receiving them at par pays a Confederate Tax of 33⅓ per cent upon all monies that pass through her Treasury. This of course cannot be submitted to.

The repudiation policy of Congress, seems therefore to have left us but one alternative, and that is to receive and pay out only such issues of Confederate notes, as under the acts of Congress pass at par, without the deduction of 33⅓ or any other per cent But as we are obliged to have funds before the time when the new issues of Confederate notes can go into circulation, the question presented is, how shall we supply the Treasury in the mean time? In my judgment the proper plan will be to issue State Treasury notes, payable on the 25th day of December next at the Treasury, and in each of the more important cities of this State, in Confederate Treasury notes, of such issue as may be made after 1st April next, to be used as circulating medium. This enables the State to anticipate the new issues, and use them in advance of their circulation by Confederate authority. The new Georgia Treasury notes of this issue, would be just as good as the new issue of Confederate notes; because payable in them; and would be as current in payment of debts. The act should provide that all taxes hereafter due the State for this year, shall be payable in the Confederate Treasury notes of the new issue, and that they shall be deposited in the Treasury when collected, to redeem the State notes payable in them. The act should also provide that the State notes shall be returned, and the Confederate notes received in place of them within three months after they are due, or that the State will no longer be liable for their payment. This would prevent holders from laying them away, and refusing to bring them in for payment when due, according to the terms of the contract. As the State tax is not due until next fall, there will be an abundant supply of the new Confederate notes in circulation by that time, to obviate all difficulty in obtaining them by our people to pay the tax.

I recommend the passage of a joint resolution authorizing the Governor to have funded in the six per cent bonds, provided for by the act of Congress, all Confederate notes which may remain in the Treasury, or may be in the hands of any of the financial agents of the State, after the first day of April next, and to sell and dispose of such bonds at their market value in currency, which can be made available in payments to be made by the Treasury, and to credit the Treasurer with any losses that may accrue by reason of the failure of the bonds to bring par in the market.

ORPHANS' ESTATES.

On account of the present depreciated value of the Confederate securities, I recommend the repeal of the law which authorizes Executors, Administrators and Trustees to invest the funds of those whom they represent in these securities. As the law stands, it enables unscrupulous fiduciary agents to perpetrate frauds upon innocent orphans, and other helpless persons represented by them, and in effect compels orphans, and those represented by trustees, to invest their whole estates in government bonds, which no other class is required to do.

FURLOUGHS REFUSED.

On the 27th of February, when I issued my Proclamation, calling you into extra session, I telegraphed the Secretary of War, and asked that furloughs be granted to members in military service, to attend the session, and received a reply stating that it had "been concluded not to grant furloughs to attend the session," that, "officers so situated are entitled to resign and may so elect."

I regret this determination of the Confederate government, as it places our gallant officers who have been elected by the people to represent them, and to whom, as well as their predecessors similarly situated, furloughs were never before denied, in a position where it costs them their commissions to attempt to discharge their duties as Representatives of the people.

THE NEW MILITIA ORGANIZATION AND CONSCRIPTION.

Since your adjournment in December, the Adjutant and Inspector General, under my direction, has done all in his power to press forward the organization of the militia of the State, in conformity to the act passed for that purpose; and I have the pleasure to state, that the enrollments are generally made, except in a few localities, where proximity to the enemy has prevented it; and the organizations will soon be completed.

At this stage in our proceedings, we are met with formidable obstacles, thrown in our way by the late act of Congress, which subjects those between 17 and 50 to enrollment as Conscripts, for Confederate service. This act of Congress proposes to take from the State. as was done on a former occasion, her entire military force, who belong to the active list, and to leave her without a force, in the different counties, sufficient to execute her laws or suppress servile insurrection.

Our Supreme Court has ruled, that the Confederate government has the power to raise armies by conscription, but it has not decided that it also has the power to enroll the whole population of the State who remain at home, so as to place the whole people under the military control of the Confederate government, and thereby take from the States all command over their own citizens, to execute their own laws, and place the internal police regulations of the States in the hands of the President. It is one thing to "raise armies", and another, and quite a different thing, to put the whole population at home under military law, and compel every man to obtain a military detail, upon such terms as the central government may dictate, and to carry a military pass in his pocket while he cultivates his farm, or attends to his other necessary avocations at home.

Neither a planter nor an overseer engaged upon the farm, nor a blacksmith making agricultural implements. nor a miller grinding for the people at home, belongs to, or constitutes any part of the armies of the Confederacy; and there is not the shadow of Constitutional power, vested in the Confederate government, for conscribing and putting these classes, and others engaged in home pursuits, under military rule, while they remain at home to discharge these duties. If conscription were constitutional as a means of raising armies by the Confederate government, it could not be constitutional to conscribe those not *actually* needed, and to be *employed* in the army, and the constitutional power to "raise armies", could never carry with it the power in Congress to conscribe the whole people, who are not needed for the armies, but are left at home, because more useful there, and place them under military government and compel them to get military details to plough in their fields, shoe their farm horses, or to go to mill.

Conscription carried to this extent, is the essence of military despotism ; placing all civil rights, in a state of subordination to military power, and putting the personal freedom of each individual, in civil life, at the will of the chief of the military power. But it may be said that conscription may act upon one class as legally as another, and that all classes are equally subject to it. This is undoubtedly true. If the government has a right to conscribe at all, it has a right to conscribe persons of all classes, till it has raised enough to supply its armies. But it has no right to go farther and conscribe all, who are, by its own consent, to remain at home to make supplies. If it considers supplies necessary, somebody must make them, and those who do it, being no part of the army, should be *exempt* from conscription, and the annoyance of military dictation, while engaged in civil, and not military pursuits.

If all between 17 and 50 are to be enrolled and placed in constant military service, we must conquer the enemy while we are consuming our present crop of provisions, or we are ruined ; as it will be impossible for the old men over 50, and the boys under 17, to make supplies enough to feed our armies and people another year. I think every practical man in the Confederacy who knows anything about our agricultural interests and resources, will readily admit this.

If, on the other hand, it is not the intention to put those between 17 and 18, and between 45 and 50, into service, as *soldiers*, but to leave them at home to produce supplies, and occasionally to do police and other duties, within the State, which properly belong to the militia of a State ; or in other words, if it is the intention simply to take the control of them from the State, so as to deprive her of all power, and leave her without sufficient force to execute her own laws, or suppress servile insurrection, and place the whole militia of the State, not needed for constant service, in the Confederate armies, under the control of the President, while engaged in their civil pursuits, the act is unconstitutional and oppressive, and ought not to be executed.

If the act is executed in this State, it deprives her of her whole *active* militia, as Congress has so shaped it as to include the identical persons embraced in the act passed at your late session, and to transfer the control of them all from the State to the Confederate government.

The State has already enrolled these persons under the solemn act of her Legislature, for her own defense, and it is a question for you to determine, whether the necessities of the State, her sovereignty and dignity, and justice to those who are to be affected by the act, do not forbid that she should permit her organization to be broken up, and her means of self-preservation to be taken out of her hands. If this is done, what will be our condition? I prefer to answer by adopting the language of the present able and patriotic Governor of Virginia: "A sovereign State without a soldier, and without the dignity of strength—stripped of all her men, and with only the form and pageantry of power —would indeed be nothing more than a wretched dependency, to which I should grieve to see our proud old Commonwealth reduced."

I may be reminded that the enemy has three times as many white men, able to bear arms, as we have, and that it is necessary to take all between the ages above mentioned, or we cannot keep as many men in the field as he does.

If the result depended upon our ability to do this, we must necessarily fail. But, fortunately for us, this is not the case. While they have the advantage in numbers, we have other advantages which, if properly improved, they can never overcome. We are the invaded party, in the right, struggling for all we have, and for all that we expect our posterity to inherit. This gives us great moral advantage over a more powerful enemy, who, as the invaders, are in the wrong, and are fighting for conquest and power: We have the inner and shorter lines of defense, while they have the longer and much more difficult ones. For instance, if we desire to reinforce Dalton from Wilmington, Charleston, Savannah, and Mobile, or to reinforce either of those points from Dalton, we can do so by throwing troops rapidly over a short line from one point to the other. If the enemy wishes to reinforce Charleston or Chattanooga from Washington or New Orleans, he must throw his troops a long distance around, almost upon the circumference of a circle, while we meet them with our reinforcements by throwing them across the diameter of a semicircle. This difference in our favor is as great as four to one, and enables us, if our troops are properly handled, to repel their assaults with little more than one-fourth their number.

In consideration of these and numerous other advantages which an invaded people, united and determined to be free, always has, it is not wise policy for us to undertake to keep in the field as large a number as the enemy has.

It is the duty of those in authority in a country, engaged in a war which calls for all the resources at command, to consider well what proportion of the whole population can safely be kept under arms. In our present condition, surrounded by the enemy and our ports blockaded, so that we can place but little dependence upon foreign supplies, we are obliged to keep a sufficient number of men in the agricultural fields, to make supplies for our troops under arms and their families at home, or we must ultimately fail.

The policy which would compel all our men to go to the military field, and leave our farms uncultivated and our workshops vacant, would be the most fatal and unwise that could be adopted. In that case, the enemy need only avoid battle and continue the war till we consume the supplies now on hand, and we would be completely in their power.

There is a certain proportion of a people in our condition who can remain under arms, and the balance of the population at home can support them. So long as that proportion has not been reached, more may be safely taken; but when it is reached, every man taken from the field of production, and placed as a consumer in the military field, makes us that much weaker; and if we go far beyond the proportion, failure and ruin are inevitable, as the army must soon disband, when it can no longer be supplied with the necessaries of life.. There is reason to fear that those in authority have not made safe calculations upon this point, and that they do not fully appreciate the incalculable importance of the agricultural interests in this struggle.

We are able to keep constantly under arms two hundred thousand effective men, and to support and maintain that force, by our own resources and productions, for twenty years to come. No power nor State can ever be conquered so long as it can maintain that number of good troops. If the enemy should bring a million against us, let us remember, that there is such a thing as whipping the fight without fighting it; and. avoiding pitched battles and unnecessary collisions, let us give this vast force time to melt away under the heat of summer and the snows of winter, as did Xerxes' army in Greece, and Napoleon's in Russia, and the enemy's resources and strength will exhaust when so prodigally used, much more rapidly than ours when properly economised. In properly economising our strength and husbanding our resources, lie our best hope of success.

Instead of making constant new drafts upon the agricultural and mechanical labor of the country for recruits for the army, to swell our numbers beyond our present muster rolls, which must prove our ruin if our provisions fail, I respectfully submit that it would be wiser to *put the troops into the army*, and leave men enough at home to support them. In other words, compel the thousands of young officers in gold lace and brass buttons, who are constantly seen crowding our railroads and hotels, many of whom can seldom be found at their posts, and thousands of straggling soldiers who are absent without leave, or by the favoritism of officers, whose names are on the pay rolls, and who are not producers at home, to remain at their places in the army. This is justice alike to the country, to the tax-payers, to the gallant officers who stand firmly at the post of duty, and the gallant soldiers who seldom or never get furloughs, but are always in the thickest of the fight. When they are enduring and suffering so much, why should the favorites of power and those of their comrades who seek to avoid duty and danger, be countenanced or tolerated at home, while their names stand upon the muster rolls?

If all who are able for duty, and who are now nominally in service drawing pay from the Government, are compelled to do their duty faithfully, there will be no need of compelling men over 45 to leave their homes, or of disbanding the State militia to place more men under the President's control.

CONFLICT WITH THE CONFEDERATE GOVERNMENT.

But it may be said that an attempt to maintain the rights of the State will produce conflict with the Confederate Government. I am aware that there are those who, from motives not necessary to be here mentioned, are ever ready to raise the cry of *conflict*, and to criticise and condemn the action of Georgia, in every case where her constituted authorities protest against the encroachments of the central power, and seek to maintain her dignity and sovereignty as a State, and the constitutional rights and liberties of her people.

Those who are unfriendly to State sovereignty, and desire to consolidate all power in the hands of the Confederate Government, hoping to promote their undertaking by operating upon the fears of the timid, after each new aggression upon the constitutional rights of the States, fill the newspaper presses with the cry of *conflict*, and warn the people to beware of those who seek to maintain their constitutional rights, as *agitators* or *partisans* who may embarrass the Confederate Government in the prosecution of the war.

Let not the people be deceived by this false clamor. It is the same cry of *conflict* which the Lincoln Government raised against all who defended the rights of the Southern States against its tyranny. It is the cry which the usurpers of power have ever raised against those who rebuke their encroachments and refuse to yield to their aggressions.

When did Georgia embarrass the Confederate Government in any matter pertaining to the vigorous prosecution of the war? When did she fail to furnish more than her full quota of troops, when she was called upon as a State by the proper Confederate authority? And when did her gallant sons ever quail before the enemy, or fail nobly to illustrate her character upon the battle field?

She can not only repel the attacks of her enemies on the field of deadly conflict, but she can as proudly repel the assaults of those who, ready to bend the knee to power for position and patronage, set themselves up to criticise her conduct; and she can confidently challenge them to point to a single instance in which she has failed to fill a requisition for troops made upon her through the regular constitutional channel. To the very last requisition made, she responded with over double the number required.

She stands ready at all times to do her whole duty to the

cause and to the Confederacy, but while she does this, she will never cease to require that her constitutional rights be respected, and the liberties of her people preserved. While she deprecates all conflict with the Confederate Government, if to require these be *conflict*, the *conflict* will never end till the object is attained.

"For freedom's battle once begun,
Bequeath'd by bleeding sire to son,
Though battle I oft is ever won,"

will be emblazoned in letters of living light upon her proud banners, until State sovereignty and constitutional liberty, as well as Confederate independence, are firmly established.

SUSPENSION OF THE HABEAS CORPUS.

I cannot withhold the expression of the deep mortification I feel at the late action of Congress, in attempting to suspend the privilege of the writ of *Habeas Corpus*, and to confer upon the President powers expressly denied to him by the Constitution of the Confederate States. Under pretext of a *necessity* which our whole people know does not exist in this case, whatever may have been the motives, our Congress, with the assent, and at the *request* of the Executive, has struck a fell blow at the liberties of these States.

The Constitution of the Confederate States declares that, " The privilege of the writ of *habeas corpus* shall not be suspended, unless when in cases of rebellion or invasion the public safety may require it." The power to suspend 'the *habeas corpus* at all, is derived, not from express and direct delegation, but from implication only, and an implication can never be raised in opposition to an express restriction. In case of any conflict between the two, an implied power must always yield to express restrictions upon its exercise. The power to suspend the privilege of the writ of *habeas corpus* derived by implication, must therefore be always limited by the *express* declaration in the Constitution that :

"The right of the people to be secure in their *persons*, houses, papers, and effects, against unreasonable searches and seizures *shall not be violated*; and *no warrants shall issue* but upon probable cause, supported by *oath or affirmation*, and particularly describing the place to be searched and the *persons* or things to be seized," and the further declaration that, "no person shall be deprived of life, *liberty* or property, without due process of law." And that,

"In *all criminal prosecutions* the accused shall enjoy the right of a *speedy* and public trial by an *impartial jury* of the State or District where the crime shall have been committed, which district shall have been previously ascertained by law, and to be informed of the nature and cause of the accusation ; to be confronted with the witnesses against him ; to have compulsory process for obtaining witnesses in his favor ; and to have the assistance of counsel for his defense."

Thus it is an express guaranty of the Constitution, that the "*persons*" of the people shall be secure, and "*no warrants* shall issue," but upon probable cause, supported by *oath* or *affirmation*," particularly describing "the *persons* to be seized;" that, "no *person* shall be deprived of *liberty*, without due process of law", and that, in "all criminal prosecutions" the accused shall enjoy the right of a *speedy* and *public* trial, by an *impartial jury*."

The Constitution also defines the *powers* of the Executive, which are limited to those delegated, among which there is no one, authorizing him to issue *warrants* or *order arrests* of persons not in *actual* military service ; or to sit as a judge in any case, to try any person for a criminal offense, or to appoint any *court* or *tribunal* to do it, not provided for in the Constitution, as part of the judiciary. The power to *issue warrants* and try persons under criminal accusations are *judicial* powers, which belong, under the Constitution, *exclusively* to the *judiciary* and not to the *Executive*. His power to order arrests, as Commander-in-Chief, is strictly a *military* power, and is confined to the arrest of *persons subject to military power*, as to the arrest of persons in the army or navy of the Confederate States ; or in the Militia, when in the *actual* service of the Confederate States, and does not extend to any persons in civil life, unless they be followers of the camp, or within the lines of the army. This is clear from that provision of the Constitution which declares, that,

"No person shall be held to answer for a capital, or otherwise infamous crime, unless on a *presentment* or *indictment* of a *grand jury*, execept in cases arising *in the land or naval forces*, or *in the militia*, when in *actual service* in time of war or public danger." But even here, the power of the President as Commander-in-Chief, is not absolute, as his powers and duties, in ordering arrests of persons, in the land or naval forces, or in the militia, when in *actual* service, are clearly defined by the rules and articles of war, prescribed by Congress. *Any warrant* issued by the President, or *any arrest* made by him, or under his order, of *any person* in civil life and not subject to military command, is *illegal* and in *plain violation of the Constitution* ; as it is impossible for Congress, by implication, to confer upon the President the right to exercise powers of arrest, expressly forbidden to him by the Constitution. Any effort, on the part of Congress, to do this, is but an attempt to revive the odious practice of ordering political arrests, or issuing letters *de cachet* by royal prerogative, so long since renounced by our English ancestors ; and the denial of the right of the constitutional judiciary to investigate such cases, and the provision for creating a court appointed by the Executive, and changeable at his will, to take jurisdiction of the same, are in violation of the great principles of *Magna Charta*, the Bill of Rights, the

2

habeas corpus act, and the Constitution of the Confederate States, upon which both English and American liberty rest; and are but an attempt to revive the odious Star-Chamber court of England, which, in the hands of wicked kings, was used for tyranical purposes, by the crown, until it was finally abolished by act of parliament, of 16th Charles the first, which went into operation on the first of August 1641. · This act has ever since been regarded as one of the great bulwarks of English liberty ; and as it was passed by the English Parliament to secure our English ancestors against the very same character of arbitrary arrests which the late act of Congress is intended to authorize the President to make, I append ¦a copy of it to this message, with the same italics and small capital letters, which are used in the printed copy in the book from which it is taken. It will be seen that the court of " Star-Chamber," which was the instrument in the hands of the English king, for *investigating* his illegal arrests and carrying out his arbitrary decrees, was much more respectable, on account of the character, learning and ability of its members, than the Confederate Star-Chamber, or court of "proper officers," which the act of Congress gives the President power to appoint, to *investigate* his illegal arrests.

I am aware of no instance in which the British king has ordered the arrest of any person in civil life, in any other manner than by judicial warrant, issued by the established courts of the realm, and in which he has suspended, or attempted to suspend the privilege of the writ of *habeas corpus*, since the Bill of Rights and act of settlement passed in 1689. To attempt this in 1864 would cost the present reigning Queen no less price than her crown.

The only suspension of the privilege of the writ of *habeas corpus*, known to our Constitution, and compatible with the provisions already stated, goes to the simple extent of preventing the release, under it, of persons whose arrests have been ordered under constitutional warrants from judicial authority. To this extent the Constitution allows the suspension, in case of rebellion or invasion, in order that the accused may be certainly and safely held for trial ; but Congress has no right, under pretext of exercising this power, to authorize the President to make *illegal arrests*, prohibited by the Constitution ; and when Congress has attempted to confer such powers on the President, if he should order such illegal arrests, it would be the imperative duty of the judges, who have solemnly sworn to support the Constitution, to disregard such unconstitutional legislation, and grant relief to persons so illegally imprisoned ; and it would be the duty of the Legislative and Executive departments of the States to sustain and protect the judiciary in the discharge of this obligation.

By an examination of the act of Congress, now under

consideration, it will be seen that it is not an act to suspend the privilege of the writ of *habeas corpus* in case of warrants issued by *judicial authority;* but the main purpose of the act seems to be to authorize the President to issue warrants, supported by neither *oath* nor *affirmation*, and to make arrests of persons not in military service, upon charges of a nature proper for investigation in the judicial tribunals only, and to prevent the Courts from inquiring into such arrests, or granting relief against such illegal usurpations of power, which are in direct and palpable violation of the Constitution.

The act enumerates more than twenty different causes of arrest, most of which are cognizable, and tryable only in the judicial tribunals established by the Constitution ; and for which *no warrants* can legally issue for the arrest of persons in civil life, by any power except the judiciary, and then only upon probable cause, supported by *oath* or *affirmation*, particularly describing the *persons* to be seized ; such as "treason" "treasonable efforts or combinations to subvert the Government of the Confederate States," "conspiracies to overthrow the Government." or " conspiracies to resist the lawful authority of the Confederate States," giving the enemy " aid and comfort", " attempts to incite servile insurrection," " the burning of bridges," "Railroad," or "Telegraph lines," "harboring deserters," and "other offences against the laws of the Confederate States," &c., &c. And as if to place the usurpation of power beyond doubt or cavil, the act expressly declares that the "suspension shall apply only to the case of persons, *arrested or detained by the President,* the Secretary of War, or the General officer commanding the Trans Mississippi Military Department, *by authority and under the control of the President,*" in the cases enumerated in the act, most of which are exclusively of judicial cognizance, and in which cases *the President* has not the shadow of Constitutional authority to *issue warrants* or order arrests, but is actually prohibited by the Constitution from doing so.

This then is not an act to suspend the privilege of the writ of *habeas corpus,* in the manner authorized by implication by the Constitution ; but it is an act to authorize the President to make *illegal and unconstitutional arrests,* in cases which the Constitution gives to the judiciary, and denies to the Executive ; and to prohibit all judicial interference for the relief of the citizen, when tyranized over by illegal arrest, under letters *de cachet* issued by Executive authority.

Instead of the legality of the arrest being examined in the judicial tribunals appointed by the Constitution, it is to be examin d in the Confederate Star Chamber; that is, by *officers* appointed by the President. Why say that the "*President shall cause proper officers* to investigate" the legality of arrests ordered by him ? Why not permit the Judges, whose constitutional right and duty it is to do it ?

We are witnessing with too much indifference assumptions of power by the Confederate Government which in ordinary times would arouse the whole country to indignant rebuke and stern resistance. History teaches us that submission to one encroachment upon conssitutional liberty is always followed by another ; and we should not forget that important rights, yielded to those in power, without rebuke or protest, are never recovered by the people without revolution.

If this act is acquiesed in, the President, the Secretary of War, and the commander of the Trans Mississippi department under the control of the President, each has the power conferred by Congress, to imprison whomsoever he chooses ; and it is only necessary to *allege* that it is done on account of "treasonable efforts" or of "conspiracies to resist the lawful authority of the Confederate States," or for "giving aid and comfort to the enemy," or other of the causes of arrest enumerated in the Statute, and have a subaltern to file his affidavit accordingly, *after the arrest* if a writ of habeas corpus is sued out, and no Court dare inquire into the cause of the imprisonment. The Statute makes the President and not the courts the judge of the sufficiency of the cause for his own acts. Either of you or any other citizen of Georgia, may at any moment (as Mr. Vallandigham was in Ohio) be dragged from your homes at midnight by armed force, and imprisoned at the will of the President, upon the pretext that you have been guilty of some offense of the character above named, and no court known to our judiciary can inquire into the wrong or grant relief.

When such bold strides towards military despotism and absolute authority, are taken, by those in whom we have confided, and who have been placed in high official position to guard and protect constitutional and personal liberty, it is the duty of every patriotic citizen to sound the alarm, and of the State Legislatures to say, in thunder tones, to those · who assume to govern us by absolute power, that there is a point beyond which freemen will not permit encroachments to go.

The Legislatures of the respective States are looked to as the guardians of the rights of those whom they represent, and it is their duty to meet such dangerous encroachments upon the liberties of the people, promptly. and express their unqualified condemnation, and to instruct their Senators, and request their Representatives to repeal this most monstrous act, or resign a trust, which, by permitting it to remain on the statute book, they abuse, to the injury of those who have honored them with their confidence in this trying period of our history. I earnestly recommend that the Legislature of this State take prompt action upon this subject, and stamp the act with the seal of their indignant rebuke.

Can the President no longer trust the judiciary with the exercise of the legitimate powers conferred upon it by the Constitution and laws? In what instance have the grave and dignified Judges proved disloyal or untrue to our cause? When have they embarrassed the government, by turning loose traitors, skulkers or spies? Have they not, in every instance, given the Government the benefit of their doubts in sustaining its action, though they might thereby seem to encroach upon the rights of the States, and for a time deny substantial justice to the people? Then why this implied censure upon them?

What justification exists now for this most monstrous deed, which did not exist during the first or second year of the war, unless it be found in the fact, that those in power have found the people ready to submit to every encroachment, rather than make an issue with the Government, while we are at war with the enemy, and have, on that account, been emboldened to take the step which is intended to make the President as absolute in his power of arrest and imprisonment, as the Czar of all the Russias? What reception would the members of Congress, from the different States, have met in 1861, had they returned to their constituents and informed them that they had suspended the *habeas corpus*, and given the President the power to imprison the people of these States, with no restraint upon his sovereign will? Why is liberty less sacred now than it was in 1861? And what will we have gained when we have achieved our Independence of the Northern States, if in our effort to do so, we have permitted our form of government to be subverted, and have lost *Constitutional liberty* at home?

The hope of the country now rests in the new Congress, soon to assemble. They must maintain our liberties against encroachment, and wipe this, and all such stains, from the statute book, or the Sun of liberty will soon set in darkness and blood.

Let the constituted authorities of each State, send up to their Representatives, when they assemble in Congress, an unqualified demand for prompt redress; or a return of the commissions which they hold from their respective States.

THE CAUSES OF THE WAR, HOW CONDUCTED, AND WHO RESPONSIBLE.

Cruel, bloody, desolating war is still waged against us by our relentless enemies, who, disregarding the laws of nations and the rules of civilized warfare, whenever either interferes with their fanatical objects or their interest, have in numerous instances been guilty of worse than savage cruelty.

They have done all in their power to burn our cities, when unable by their skill and valor to occupy them; and to turn innocent women and children, who may have escaped death by the shells thrown among them, without previous notice, into the streets, destitute of homes, food and clothing.

They have devastated our country, wherever their unhallowed feet have trod our soil, burning and destroying factories, mills, agricultural implements, and other valuable property.

They have cruelly treated our sons while in captivity, and in violation of a cartel agreed upon, have refused to exchange them with us, for their own soldiers, unless we would consent, against the laws of nations, to exchange our slaves as belligerents, when induced or forced by them, to take up arms against us.

They have done all in their power to incite our slaves to insurrection and murder, and when unable to seduce them from their loyalty, have, when they occupied our country, compelled them to engage in war against us.

They have robbed us of our negro women and children who were comfortable contented and happy with their owners, and under pretext of extraordinary philanthropy, have in the name of liberty congregated thousands of them together in places where they could have neither the comforts nor the necessaries of life, there neglected and despised to die by pestilence and hunger.

In numerous instances their brutal soldiers have violated the persons of our innocent and helpless women; and have desecrated the graves of our ancestors and polluted and defiled the altars which we have dedicated to the worship of the living God.

In addition to these and other enormities hundreds of thousands of valuable lives, both North and South, have been sacrificed, causing the shriek of the mother, the wail of the widow and the cry of the orphan to ascend to Heaven from almost every hearthstone in all the broad land once known as the United States.

Such is but a faint picture of the devastation, cruelty and bloodshed which have marked this struggle.

War in is most mitigated form, when conducted according to the rules established by the most enlightened and civilized nations, is a terrible scourge and cannot exist without the most enormous guilt resting upon the heads of those who have without just cause brought it upon the innocent and helpless people who are its unfortunate victims. Guilt may rest in unequal degrees in a struggle like this upon both parties, but both cannot be innocent. Where then rests this crushing load of guilt?

While I trust I shall be able to show that it rests not upon the people nor rulers of the South, I do not claim that it rested at the commencement of the struggle upon the whole people of the North.

There was a large intelligent and patriotic portion of the people of the Northern States, led by such men as

23

Pierce, Douglas, Vallandingham, Bright, Voorhies, Pugh, Seymour, Wood and many other honored names, who did all in their power to rebuke and stay the wicked reckless fanaticism which precipitated the two sections into this terrible conflict. With such men as these in power we might have lived together in the Union perpetually.

In addition to the strength of the Democratic party in the North, there were a large number of persons whose education had brought them into sympathy with the so called Republican, or in other words the old federal, consolidation party, who would never have followed the wicked leaders of that party who used the slavery question as an hobby upon which to ride into power, and who to-day stand before Heaven and earth guilty of shedding the blood of hundreds of thousands and destroying the brightest hopes of posterity, had they known the true objects of their leaders and the results which must follow the triumph of their policy at the ballot box.

The moral guilt of this war rested then in its incipiency neither upon the people of the South nor upon the Democratic party of the North, or upon that part of the Republican party who were deluded and deceived. But it rested upon the heads of the wicked leaders of the Republican party, who had refused to be bound by the compacts of the Constitution made by our common ancestry. These men when in power in the respective States of the North arrayed themselves in open hostility against an important provision of the Constitution, for the security of clearly expressed and unquestionable rights of the people of the Southern States.

Many of the more fanatical of them denounced the Constitution, because of its protection of the property of the slaveholder, as a "covenant with death and a league with Hell," and refusing to be bound by it, declared that a "higher law" was the rule of their conduct, and appealed to the Bible as that "higher law." But when the precepts of God in favor of slavery were found in both the old and the new testament, they repudiated the Bible and its Divine Author and declared for an *anti-Slavery Bible and an anti-Slavery God.*

The abolition party having when in power, in their respective States, set at naught that part of the Constitution which guarantees protection to the rights and property of the Southern people, and having by fraud and misrepresentation obtained possession of the federal government, the Southern people in self-defence were compelled to leave the Union in which their rights were no longer respected. Having destroyed the Union by their wicked acts and their bad faith, these leaders rallied a majority of the people of the North to their support, with a promise to restore it again *by force.* Monstrous paradox! that a Union which was formed upon a compact between sovereign States, being eminently a creature of consent, is to be upheld *by force.* But monstrous as it is, the war springs ostensibly from this source—this is its origin, its soul and its life, so far as a shadow of pretext for it can be found. In their mad effort to restore by force a Union which they have destroyed, and to save themselves from the just vengeance which awaited them for their crimes, the abolition leaders in power have lighted up the continent with a blaze of war which has destroyed hundreds of millions of dollars worth of property, and hundreds of thousands of valuable lives, and loaded posterity with a debt which must cause wretchedness and poverty for generations to come. And all for what? That fanaticism might triumph over constitutional liberty as achieved by the great men of 1776, and that ambitious men might have place and power. In their efforts to destroy our liberties the people of the North, if successful, would inevitably lose their own by overturning, as they are now attempting to do, the great principles of Republicanism upon which constitutional liberty rests. The government in the hands of the abolition administration is now a despotism as absolute as that of Russia.

Unoffending citizens are seized in their beds at night by armed force, and dragged to dungeons and incarcerated at the will of the tyrant, because they have dared to speak for constitutional liberty and to protest against military despotism.

The *Habeas Corpus* that great bulwark of liberty, without which no people can be secure in their lives persons or property, which cost the English several bloody wars and which was finally wrung from the crown by the sturdy Barons and people at the point of the bayonet; which has ever been the boast of every American patriot, and which I pray God may never, under pretext of *military necessity,* be yielded to encroachments by the people of the South, has been trampled under foot by the Government at Washington which imprisons at its pleasure whomsoever it will.

The freedom of the ballot box has also been destroyed, and the elections have been carried by the overawing influence of military force.

Under pretext of keeping men enough in the field to subdue the South, President Lincoln takes care to keep enough to hold the North in subjection also, to imprison or exile those who attempt to sustain their ancient rights liberties and usages, and to drive from the ballot box those who are not subservient to his will or enough of them to enable his party to carry the elections. Can an intelligent Northern Conservative man contemplate this state of things without exclaiming, whither are we drifting? What will we gain by the subjugation of the South if in our attempt to do it we must lose our own liberties and rivet upon ourselves and our posterity the chains of military despotism?

How long a people once free will submit to the despotism of such a government, the future must develop. One thing is certain, while those who now rule remain in power in Washington, the people of the *Sovereign States* of America can never adjust their difficulties. But war, bloodshed, devastation and increased indebtedness, must be the inevitable result. There must be a change of administration and more moderate councils prevail in the Northern States, before we can ever have peace. While subjugation, abolition and confiscation are the terms offered by the Federal Government, the Southern people will resist, as long as the patriotic voice of woman can stimulate a Guerilla band, or a single armed soldier to deeds of daring in defence of liberty and home.

I have said, the South is not the guilty party in this dreadful carnage, and I think it not inappropriate that the reasons should be often repeated at the bar of an intelligent public opinion, that our own people and the world should have "line upon line," "precept upon precept," "here a little and there a little," "in season and out of season," as some may suppose, to show the true nature of this contest—the principles involved—the objects of the war on our side, as well as that of the enemy, that all right minded men everywhere may see and understand, that *this contest is not of our seeking*, and that we have had no wish or desire to injure those who war against us, except so far as has been necessary for the protection and preservation of ourselves. Our sole object from the beginning has been to defend, maintain and preserve our ancient usages, customs, liberties and institutions, as achieved and established by our ancestors in the revolution of 1776.

That Revolution was undertaken to establish two great rights—State Sovereignty—and self government. Upon these the Declaration of Independence was predicated, and they were the Corner Stone upon which the Constitution rested. The denial of these two great principles cost Great Britian her American Colonies which had so long been her pride. And the denial of them by the Government at Washington, if persisted in, must cost the people of the United States the liberties of themselves and their posterity. These are the pillars upon which the temple of Constitutional liberty stands, and if the Northern people in their mad effort to destroy the Sovereignty of the Southern States, and take from our people the rights of self-government, should be able, with the strength of an ancient Sampson, to lay hold upon the pillars and overturn the edifice, they must necessarily be crushed beneath its ruins, as the destruction of State Sovereignty and the right of self-government in the Southern States, by the agency of the

Federal Government, necessarily involves the like destruction in the Northern States; as no people can maintain these rights for themselves who will shed the blood of their neighbors to destroy them in others. It is impossible for half the States of a Confederacy, if they assist the central government to destroy the rights and liberties of the other half, to maintain their own rights and liberties against the central power, after it has crushed their Co-States.

The two great truths announced by Mr. Jefferson, in the Declaration of Independence, and concurred in by all the great men of the revolution were, 1st, "That Governments derive their just powers from the *consent of the Governed.*" 2nd, "That these United Colonies are, and of right ought to be, *free* and *independent States.*"

We are not to understand by the first great truth, that each individual member of the aggregate mass composing the State, must give his consent before he can be justly governed; or that the consent of each, or a particular class of individuals in a State is necessary. By the "governed" is evidently here meant communities and bodies of men capable of organizing and maintaining government. The "consent of the governed," refers to the aggregate will of the community or State in its organized form, and expressed through its legitimate and properly constituted organs.

In elaborating this great truth, Mr. Jefferson, in the Declaration of Independence, says, that governments are instituted among men to secure certain "inalienable rights," that "among these are life, liberty and the pursuit of happiness;" "that whenever any form of government becomes destructive of these ends, it is the right of the people to alter or abolish it, and to institute a new government, laying its foundation on such principles, and organizing its powers in such form, as to them shall seem most likely to effect their safety and happiness."

According to this great fundamental principle, the *Sovereign States* of America, North and South, can only be governed by their own consent, and whenever the Government to which they have given their consent, becomes destructive of the great ends for which it was formed, they have a perfect right to "abolish it" by withdrawing their consent from it, as the Colonies did from the British Government, and to form a "new Government," with its foundations laid on such principles, and its powers organized in such form as to them shall seem most likely to effect their safety and happiness." Upon the application, to the present controversy, of this great principle, to which the Northern States are firmly committed as the Southern States, Georgia can proudly challenge New York to trial before the the bar of enlightened public opinion, and impartial history must write the verdict in her favor, and triumphantly vindicate her action in the course she has pursued.

Not only the Sovereign States of America have heretofore recognized this great truth, but it has been recognized by the able and enlightened Emperor of the French, who owes his present elevation to the "consent of the governed."

He was called to the Presidency by the free suffrage or consent of the French people, and when he assumed the imperial title, he again submitted the question to the "governed" at the ballot box, and they gave their "consent."

At the recent treaty of peace with the Emperor of Austria, he ceded an Austrian province to France, and Napoleon refused to "govern it," till the people at the ballot box gave "their consent" that he should do so.

The Northern States of America are to-day, through the agency of the despotism at Washington, waging a bloody war upon the Southern States, to crush out this great American principle, announced, and maintained in a seven years war, by our common ancestry, after it had won the approbation of the ablest and most enlightened Sovereign of Europe.

In discussing this great principle, I can but remark, how strange is the contrast between the conduct of the Emperor Napoleon, and that of President Lincoln. Napoleon refuses to govern a province till a majority of the people at the ballot box has given their consent. Lincoln, after having done all in his power to destroy the freedom and purity of the ballot box, announces in his late proclamation his determination to govern the Sovereign States of the South *by force,* and to recognize and maintain as the government of these States, not those who at the ballot box can obtain the "consent of the governed," or of a majority of the people, but those who can obtain the consent of *one tenth* of the people of the State. Knowing that he can never govern these States with "the consent of the governed," he tramples the declaration of Independence under his feet, and proclaims to the world, that he will govern these States, not by the "consent of the governed", but by military power, so soon as he can find *one tenth* of the governed humiliated enough to give their consent.

But the world must be struck with the absurdity of the pretext upon which he bases this extraordinary pretension. He says, in substance, the Constitution requires him to guarantee to each State a republican form of government. And for the purpose of carrying out this provision of the Constitution, he proclaims that, so soon as *one tenth* of the people of each of the seceded States shall be found abject enough to take an oath to support his *unconstitutional acts,* and at the same time to support the Constitution, and shall do this monstrous deed, he will permit them to organize a State Government, and will recognize them as the Government of the State, and their officers as the regularly constituted authorities of the State. These he will aid in putting

2S

down, driving out, expelling and exterminating, the other *nine tenths,* if they do not likewise take the prescribed oath.

One-tenth of the people of a State put up and aided by military force to rule, govern or exterminate *nine-tenths!* And this to be done under the guise or professed object of guaranteeing republicanism! What would Washington, Jefferson, Madison, Monroe, Adams, Hancock, or even Hamilton, have said to this kind of republicanism? What say the conservative Northern statesmen of the present day, if permitted to speak? Does such a government as this derive its just powers from the "consent of the governed?" Is this their understanding of the republican government, which the United States is to guarantee to each State? If so, what guaranty have they for the freedom of their posterity? If the government at Washington guarantees such republicanism as this to Georgia in 1864, what may be her guaranty to Ohio and other Western States in 1874?

The absurdity of such a position, on constitutional principles or views, is too glaring for comment. When such terms are offered to them, well may the people of these States be nerved to defend their rights and liberties at every hazard, under every privation, and to the last extremity.

But I must notice the other great truth promulgated in the declaration of Independence—"that these United Colonies, are, and of right ought to be *free* and *independent States.*"

George the Third denied this great truth in 1776, and sent his armies into Virginia, the Carolinas, and Georgia, to crush out its advocates and maintain over the people a government which did not derive its *powers* from the "consent of the governed." President Lincoln, in 1861, has made war upon the same States and their Confederates, to crush out the same doctrine by armed force. Yet he has none of the apparent justification before the world that the British King had. The colonies had been planted, nurtured and governed by Great Britain. As States, they had never been independent and never claimed to be. This claim was set up for the first time in the declaration of Independence. Under these circumstances, there was some reason why the British Crown should resist it. But the great truth proclaimed was more powerful than the armies and navy of Great Britain.

On the 4th of July, 1776, our fathers made this declaration of the freedom and independence of the States. The revolution was fought upon this declaration, and on the 3d day of September 1783, in the treaty of peace, "His Britanic Majesty, acknowledges the said United States, to-wit: New Hampshire, Massachusetts Bay, Rhode Island and Providence Plantations, Connecticut, New York, New Jersey,

Pennsylvania, Delaware, Maryland, Virginia, North Carolina, South Carolina, and Georgia, to be *free, sovereign* and *independent States*; that he treats with them as such," &c.

On and after that day Georgia stood before the world, clad in all the habiliments, and possessed of all the attributes of sovereignty. When did Georgia lose this sovereignty? Was it by virtue of her previous compact with her sister States? Certainly not.

The Articles of Confederation between the colonies, during the struggle, set forth the objects to be attained, and the nature of the bond between the parties to it, and the separate sovereignty of each of the States a party to it, was expressly reserved. Was it when she, with the other States, formed the Constitution in 1787? Clearly not. The Constitution was a compact between the thirteen States, each of which had been recognized separately, by name, by the British King, as a *free sovereign* and *independent State.*

The objects and purposes for which the federal government was formed, were distinctly specified and were all set forth in the compact. The government created by it was limited in its powers by the grant, with an express reservation of all powers not delegated. The great attribute of *separate State Sovereignty* was not delegated. In this particular, there was no change from the Articles of Confederation; *Sovereignty* was still reserved, and abided with the States respectively. This more "perfect Union," was based upon the assumption that it was for the best interest of all the States to enter into it with the additional grant of powers and guarantees—each State being bound as a sovereign to perform and discharge to the others all the new obligations of the compact. It was so submitted to the people of the States respectively, and so acceded to by them. The States did not part with their *separate sovereignty* by the adoption of the Constitution. In that instrument all the powers delegated are specifically mentioned. Sovereignty, the greatest of all political powers, the source from which all others emanate, is not amongst those mentioned. It could not have been parted with except by grant, either expressed or clearly implied. The most degrading act a State can do is to lay down or surrender her sovereignty. Indeed it can not be done except by deed or grant. The surrender is not to be found in the Constitution amongst the expressly granted powers. It cannot be amongst those granted by implication; for by the terms of the compact none are granted by implication except such as are incidental to, or necessary and proper to execute those that are expressly granted. The incident can never be greater than the object—and if nothing in the powers expressly granted amounts to sovereignty, that which is the greatest of all powers, can not follow or be carried after a lesser one, as an incident by implication—and then to put the matter at rest forever, it is expressly declared, that the powers, not delegated, are reserved to the States respectively or to the people. Sovereignty, the great source of all power, therefore was left with the States by the compact, left where King George left it, and left where it has ever since remained, and will remain forever if the people of the States are true to themselves, and true to the great principles which their forefathers achieved at such cost of blood and treasure in the war of 1776.

The constitution was only the written contract or bond, between the sovereign States, in which the covenants were all plainly expressed, and each State as a sovereign pledged its faith to its sister States, to observe and keep these covenants. So long as each did this, all were bound by the compact. But it is a rule as well known and as universally recognized in savage as in civilized life—as well understood and as generally acquiesced in between sovereign States, as between private individuals, that when one party to a contract refuses to be bound by it, and to conform to its requirements, the other party is released from further compli ance.

Without entering into an argument to show the manner in which the Northern States had perverted the contract, and warped its terms to suit their own interest, in the enactment and enforcement of tariff laws for the protection of their industry at the expense of the South, and in the enactment of internal improvement laws, coast navigation laws, fishery laws, &c., &c., which were intended to enrich them at the expense of the people of the South, I need cite but a single instance of open, avowed, self-confessed, and even boasted, violation of the compact by the Northern States, to prove that the Southern States were released and discharged from further obligation to the Northern States, by every known rule of law, morality, or comity.

One of the express covenants in the written bond, to which the Northern States subscribed, and without which, as is clearly seen by reference to the debates in the Convention which formed the Constitution, the Southern States never would have agreed to or formed the compact, was in these words :

"No person held to service or labor in one State, under the laws thereof, escaping into another, shall in consequence of any *law* or *regulation therein* be discharged from such service or labor, but shall be delivered up on claim of the party to whom such service or labor may be due."

Massachusetts and other abolition States, utterly repudiated, annulled and set at naught this provision of the Constitution; and refused either to execute it or to permit the constituted authorities of the United States to carry it out, within their limits.

This shameful violation, by Massachusetts, of her plighted faith to Georgia, and this refusal to be bound by the parts of the Constitution, which she regarded burdensome to her, and unacceptable to her people, released Georgia, according to every principle of international law, from further compliance on her part. In other words, the Constitution was the bond of Union between Georgia and Massachusetts, and when Massachusetts refused longer to be bound by the Constitution, *she* thereby dissolved the union between her and Georgia.

It is truthfully said in the declaration of Independence, that "experience hath shown, that mankind are more disposed to suffer while evils are sufferable, than to right themselves by abolishing the forms to which they are accustomed." So it was with Georgia and her Southern sisters in this case. Though Massachusetts and other Northern States, by their faithless acts and repudiation of the compact, had dissolved the union existing between the States, the Southern States did not declare the dissolution ; hoping that a returning sense of justice, on the part of the Northern States, might cause them again to observe their constitutional obligations. So far from this being the case, they construed our forbearance into a consciousness of our weakness and inability to protect ourselves, and they organized a great sectional party, whose political creed was founded in injustice to the South, and whose public declarations and acts sustained the action of Massachusetts and the other faithless States.

This party, whose creed was avowed hostility to the rights of the South, triumphed in the election for President in 1860. The election of a federal Executive by a sectional party, upon a platform of avowed hostility to the constitutional rights of the South, to carry out in the Federal administration the doctrines of Massachusetts and other faithless States, left no further ground for hope that the rights of the South would longer be respected by the Northern States, which had, not only the Executive, but a majority of the Congress.

The people of the Southern States, each sovereign State acting for itself, then met in convention, and, in the most solemn manner known to our form of government, resumed the exercise of the powers which they had delegated to the common agent, now faithless to the trust reposed in it.

The right of Georgia, as a member to the original compact, to do this, is too clear for successful denial. And the right of Alabama and the other States, which had been admitted into the Union since the adoption of the Constitution, is equally incontrovertible ; as each new State came into the Union as a sovereign, upon an equal footing in all respects whatever with the original parties to the compact.

The Confederate States can therefore with confidence submit their acts to the judgment of mankind ; while with a clear conscience they appeal to a just God to maintain them in their course. They were ever true to the compact of the Union, so long as they remained members of it—their obligations under it were ever faithfully performed, and no breach of it was ever laid at their door, or truly charged against them. In exercising their undoubted right to withdraw from the Union, when the covenant had been broken by the Northern States, they sought no war—no strife. They simply withdrew from further connection with self-confessed, faithless Confederates. They offered no injury to them—threatened none—proposed none—intended none. If their previous union with the Southern States had been advantageous to them, and our withdrawal affected their interests injuriously, they ought to have been truer to their obligations. They had no just cause to complain of us; the breach of the Compact was by themselves—the vital cord of the union was severed by their own hands.

After the withdrawal of the Confederate States from the Union, if those whose gross dereliction of duty had caused it, had reconsidered their own acts, and offered new assurances for better faith in future, the question would have been fairly and justly put to the seceded States, in their sovereign capacity to determine; whether in view of their past and future interest and safety, they should renew the union with them or not; and upon what terms, and guarantees; and if they had found it to be their interest to do so, upon any terms that might have been agreed upon; on the principle assumed at the beginning, that it was for the best interest of all the States, to be bound by some Compact of union, with a Central Government of limited powers; each State faithfully performing its obligations; they would doubtless have consented to it. But if they had found it to be their interest not to do it, they would not, and ought not to have done it. For the first law of nature as applicable to States and communities, as to individuals, is self-protection and self-preservation.

Possibly a new government might have been formed at that time, upon the basis of the Germanic Confederation; with a guaranty of the complete sovereignty of all the separate States; and with a central agent or government, of more limited powers than the old one; which would have been as useful for defence against foreign aggression; and much less dangerous to the Sovereignty and the existence of the States, than the old one, when in the hands of abolition leaders, had proved itself to be.

The length of time for which the Germanic Confederation has existed, has proved, that its strength lies in what might have been considered its weakness—the separate Sovereignty of the individual members; and the very limited powers of the Central Government.

In taking the step which they were forced to do, the Southern States were careful not to provoke a conflict of arms, or any serious misunderstanding with the States that adhered to the government at Washington, as long as it was possible to avoid it. Commissioners were sent to Washington to settle and adjust all matters relating to their past connection, or joint interests and obligations, justly, honorably and peaceably. Our Commissioners were not received—they were denied the privilege of an audience—they were not heard. But they were indirectly trifled with, lied to, and misled by duplicity as infamous as that practiced by Philip of Spain towards the peace Commissioners sent by Elizabeth of England. They were detained and deceived with private assurances of a prospect of a peaceful settlement ; while the most extensive preparations were being made for war and subjugation. When they discovered this they withdrew, and the government at Washington continued its vigorous preparations to reinforce its garrisons, and hold the possession of our Forts, and to send armies to invade our territory.

Having completed his preparations for war and refused to hear any propositions for a peaceful adjustment of our difficulties, President Lincoln issued his proclamation declaring Georgia and the other seceded States to be in *rebellion*, and sent forth his armies of invasion.

In *rebellion* against whom or what ? As sovereign States have no common arbiter, to whose decision they can appeal when they are unable to settle their differences amicably, they often resort to the sword as the arbiter, and as sovereignty is always in dignity the equal of sovereignty, and a sovereign can know no superior to which allegiance is due, one sovereign may be at war with another, but one can never be in rebellion against another.

To say that the sovereign State of Georgia is in rebellion against the sovereign State of Rhode Island, is as much an absurdity as it would be to say that the sovereign State of Russia was in rebellion against the sovereign State of Great Britain in their late war. They were at war with each other ; but neither was in rebellion against the other, nor indeed could be, for neither owed any *allegiance* to the other.

Nor could one of the Sovereign States be in rebellion against the government of the United States. That government was the creature of the States, by which it was created, and they had the same power to destroy it at pleasure which they had to make it. It was their common agent with limited powers, and the States by which the agency was created had the undoubted right when it abused these powers to withdraw them. Suppose by mutual consent all the States in the Union had met in convention, each in its separate sovereign capacity, and had withdrawn all the delegated powers from the federal government, and all the States had refused to send Senators or Representatives to Congress, or to elect a President; will any sane man question their right or deny that such action of the States would have destroyed the federal government?, If so the federal government was the creature of the States and could exist only at their pleasure. It lived and breathed only by their consent. If all the parties to the compact, had the right by mutual consent to resume the powers delegated by them to the common agent; why had not part of them the right to do so, when the others violated the compact—refused to be bound longer by its obligations; and thereby released their copartners? The very fact that the States —by which it was formed, could at any time by mutual consent, disband and destroy the federal government, shows that it had no original inherent sovereignty or jurisdiction. As the creature of the States it had only such powers and jurisdictions as they gave it, and it held what it had at their pleasure. If therefore a State withdrew from the Confederacy without just cause, it was a question for the other sovereign States to consider what should be their future relations towards it; but it was a question of which the federal government had not the shadow of jurisdiction. So long as Georgia remained in the Union, if her citizens had refused to obey such laws of Congress as it had constitutional jurisdiction to pass, they might have been in rebellion against the federal government; because they resisted the authority over them, which Georgia had delegated to that government and which with her consent it still possessed. But if Georgia for just cause, of which she was the judge, chose to withdraw from the Union and resume the attributes of sovereignty, which she had delegated to the United States Government, her citizens could no longer be subject to the laws of the Union, and no longer guilty as rebels if they did not obey them.

It could be as justly said that the principal who has delegated certain limited powers to his agent in the transaction of his business, which he has afterwards withdrawn on account of their abuse by the agent, is in rebellion against the agent; or that the master is in rebellion against his servant; or the landlord against his tenant; because he has withdrawn certain privileges for a time allowed them, as that Georgia is in rebellion against her former agent the government of the United States.

These I understand to be the great fundamental doctrines of our republican form of government, so ably expounded in the Virginia and Kentucky resolutions of 1798 and 1799, which have ever since been a text book of the *true* republican party of the United States. Departure from these principles has destroyed the federal government, and been the prolific cause of all our woes. Out of this departure has sprung the doctrine of loyalty and disloyalty of the States to the federal government; from which comes ostensibly this war against us; which is itself at war with the first principles of American constitutional liberty. It involves the interests, the future safety and welfare of those States now deemed loyal, as well as those pronounced disloyal. It is the doctrine of absolutism revived in its worst form. It strikes down the essential principles of self-government, ever held so sacred in our past history, and to which all the States were indebted for their unparalleled career, in growth, prosperity and greatness, so long as those principles were adhered to and maintained inviolate.

If carried out and established, its end can be nothing but centralism and despotism. It and its fatal corollary—the policy of forcing sovereign States to the discharge of their assumed constitutional obligations, were foreshadowed by President Lincoln in his inaugural address.

Now, at the time of the delivery of that inaugural address, it was well known to him that the faithless States above alluded to, and to whose votes in the electoral college he was indebted for his election, had for years been in open, avowed and determined violation, of their constitutional obligations. This he well knew, and he also knew that the seceded States had withdrawn from the Union, because of this breach of faith on the part of the abolition States; and other anticipated violations, more dangerous, threatened from the same quarter. Yet without a word of rebuke, censure, or remonstrance, with them, for their most flagrant disloyalty to the constitution, and their disregard of their most sacred obligations under it, he then threatened and now wages war against us, on the ground of our *disloyalty*, in seeking new safe-guards for our security, when the old ones failed. And the people of those very States, whose disloyal hands had severed the ties of the Union—breaking one of the essential parts of the compact, have been, and are, his most furious myrmidons, in this most wicked and unjust crusade against us, with the view to compel the people of these so outraged States, to return to the discharge of *their* constitutional obligations! It may be gravely doubted, if the history of the world can furnish an instance of grosser perfidy or more shameful wrong.

But while the war is thus waged, professedly under the paradoxical pretext of restoring the Union, that was a creature of consent, by force; and of upholding the Constitution by coercing sovereign States; yet its real objects, as appears more obviously every day, are by no means so paradoxical. The Union under the Constitution as it was, each and every State being bound faithfully to perform and discharge its duties, and obligations, and the central government confining itself within the sphere of its limited powers, is what the authors, projectors, and controllers, of this war never wanted, and never intended, and do not now intend to maintain.

Whatever differences of opinion may have existed at the commencement, among our own people, as to the policy of secession, or the objects of the federal government, all doubt has been dispelled by the Abolition Proclamation of President Lincoln, and his subsequent action. Maddened by abolition fanaticism, and deadly hate for the white race of the South, he wages war not for the restoration of the Union—not for the support of the Constitution, but for the abolition of slavery, and the subjugation, and as he doubtless desires ultimate extermination, of the anglo-Norman race in the Southern States. Dearly beloved by him as are the African race, his acts are prompted less by love of them, than by Puritanic hate for the Cavaliers, the Huguenots, and Scotch Irish, whose blood courses freely through the veins of the white population of the South. But federal bayonets can never reverse the laws of God, which must be done, before the negro can be made the equal of the white man of the South. The freedom sought for them by the abolition party, if achieved, would result in their return to barbarism, and their ultimate extermination from the soil, where most of them were born, and were comfortable and contented, under the guardian care of the white race, before the wicked crusade was commenced.

What have been the abolition achievements of the administration? The most that has been claimed by them, is, that they have taken from their owners, and set free; 100,000 negroes. What has this cost the white race of the North and South? More than half a million of white men slain, or wrecked in health, beyond the hope of recovery, and an expenditure of not perhaps less than four thousand millions of dollars. What will it cost at this rate to liberate nearly 4,000,000 more of slaves? Northern accounts of the sickness, suffering and death, which have, under Northern treatment, carried off so large a proportion of those set free, ought to convince the most fanatical, of the cruel injury they are inflicting upon the poor helpless African.

The real objects of the war aimed at, from the beginning, were, and are not so much the deliverance of the African from bondage, as the repudiation of the great American doctrine of self-government, the subjugation of the people of these States, and the confiscation of their property. To carry out their fell purpose by misleading some simple minded folks, within their own limits, as well as ours, perhaps, they passed, in the House of Representatives of the Federal Congress, a short time since, the famous resolution:

"That as our country, and the very existence of the best government ever instituted by man, is imperilled by the most causeless and wicked rebellion, that the only hope of saving the country, and preserving this government, is by the power of the sword, we are for the most vigorous prosecution of the war, until the *Constitution and laws* shall be enforced and obeyed, in all parts of the United States ; and to that end we oppose any armistice, or intervention, or mediation, or *proposition for peace*, from any quarter, so long as there shall be found a rebel in arms against the government, and we ignore all party names, lines and issues, and recognize but two parties to this war—patriots and traitors."

Were solemn mockery, perfidious baseness, unmitigated hypocrisy, and malignant barbarity, ever more conspicuously combined, and presented for the just condemnation of a right thinking world, than they are in this resolution, passed by the abolition majority in the Lincoln Congress? Think of the members from Massachusetts and Vermont, voting for the most vigorous prosecution of the war, until the *Constitution* and *laws* shall be *enforced* and *obeyed*, in all parts of the United States. Think of the acts of the Legislature of Massachusetts, passed in 1843 and 1855, still standing upon her statute book, setting at defiance the *Constitution* and *laws*. What would become of these States, And what would become of their members themselves, who have upheld and sustained these violations of the *Constitution* and *laws*, which is the chief reason why they now hold their seats, by the votes of their constituents, if the war should be so waged? How long would it be before they would ground their arms of rebellion against the provision of the Constitution which they have set at naught, and give it their loyal support? What would become of their President and his cabinet, and all, who from the beginning of the war, and before that time, have been trampling the Constitution under their feet? Were the war waged, as they thus declare it to be their purpose to wage it, they would be the first victims of the sword, were it first turned, as it ought to be, against the first offenders. This they know full well. Obedience to the Constitution, is the last thing they want or intend. Hence the mockery, baseness, and hypocrisy, of such a declaration of purpose. On their part, it is a war of most wanton and savage aggression ; on ours, it is a war in defence of inalienable rights, in defence of everything for which freemen should live, and for which freemen may well be willing to die.

The inestimable rights of self-government, and State Sovereignty, for which their fathers, and our fathers, bled and suffered together, in the struggle with England for Independence, are the same for which we are now engaged in this most unnatural and sanguinary struggle with them. Those rights are as dear to the people of these States, as they were to those who achieved them ; and on account of the great cost of the achievement, they are the more preciously cherished by those to whom they were bequeathed, and will never be surrendered or abandoned at less sacrifice.

If no proposition for peace or armistice is to be received, or entertained, so long as we hold arms in our hands, to defend ourselves, our homes, our hearthstones, our altars, and our birthright, against such ruthless, and worse than vandal invaders, be it so! We deem it due, however, to ourselves, to the civilized world, and to those who shall come after us, to put upon record, what we are fighting for; and to let all know, who may now or hereafter, feel an interest in knowing, the real nature of this conflict, that the heavy responsibility, of such suffering, desolation, and carnage, may rest where it rightfully belongs.

It is believed that many of the people of the Northern States labor under the impression, that no propositions for peaceful adjustment have ever been made by us.

President Lincoln, in his letter to the "Unconditional Union" meeting at Springfield last summer, stated in substance, that no proposition for a peaceful adjustment of the matters in strife, had ever been made to him by those who were in control of the military forces of the Confederate States; but if any such should be made, he would entertain and give it his consideration.

This was doubtless said to make the impression on the minds of those not well informed, that the responsibility of the war was with us. This declaration of President Lincoln stands in striking contrast with that above quoted, from the republican members of the House of Representatives.

When this statement was made by President Lincoln, it was well known to him that our commissioners, sent to settle the whole matter in dispute peaceably, were refused a hearing! They were not even permitted to present their terms!

This declaration was also made soon after it was well known, throughout the Confederate States at least, that a distinguished son of this State, who is a high functionary of the government at Richmond, had consented, as military commissioner, to bear a communication in writing from President Davis, the Commander-in-Chief of our armies, to President Lincoln himself, with authority to confer upon matters therein set forth. This Commissioner, sent from the head of our armies, was not granted an audience, nor was the communication he bore received. That communication, as was afterwards known, related to divers matters connected with the general conduct of the war. Its nature however, or to what it referred, President Lincoln did not know when he refused to receive it. But from what is now known of it, if he had received it, and had heard what terms might have been proposed, for the general conduct of the war, it is reasonable to conclude, that the discussion of these, and kindred topics, might have led to some more definite ideas of the aims and objects of the war, on both sides, from which the initiative of peaceful adjustment might have sprung, unless his real purpose be, as it is believed to be, nothing short of the conquest, and subjugation of these States. His announcement, that no offer of terms of adjustment had ever been made to him, is believed to be an artful pretext on his part to cover, and hide, from the people, over whom he is assuming such absolute sway, his deep designs, first against our liberties, and then against theirs.

HOW PEACE SHOULD BE SOUGHT.

In view of these difficulties, it may be asked, when and how is this war to terminate ? It is impossible to say when it may terminate ; but it is easy to say how it will end. We do not seek to conquer the Northern people, and if we are true to ourselves they can never conquer us. We do not seek to take from them the right of self-government, or to govern them without their consent. And they have not force enough to govern us without our consent ; or to deprive us of the right to govern ourselves The blood of hundreds of thousands may yet be spilt, and the war will not still be terminated by force of arms. Negotiation *will* finally terminate it. The pen of the Statesman, more potent than the sword of the warrior, must do what the latter has failed to do.

But I may be asked, how negotiations are to commence, when President Lincoln refuses to receive commissioners sent by us ; and his Congress resolves to hear no proposition for peace ? I reply, that in my opinion, it is our duty to keep it always before the Northern people and the civilized world, that we are ready to negotiate for peace, whenever the people and government of the Northern States are prepared to recognize the great fundamental principles of the declaration of Independence, maintained by our common ancestry—the *right of all self-government and the sovereignty of the States.* In my judgment it is the duty of our government, after each important victory achieved by our gallant and glorious armies on the battle field, to make a distinct proposition to the Northern government for peace, upon these terms. By doing this, if the proposition is declined by them, we will hold them up constantly in the wrong, before their own people and the judgment of mankind. If they refuse to receive the commissioners who bear the proposition, publish it in the newspapers ; and let the conduct of their rulers be known to the people ; and there is reasonable ground to hope that the time may not be far distant when a returning sense of justice, and a desire for self-protection against despotism at home, will prompt the people of the Northern States to hurl from power those who deny the fundamental principle upon which their own liberties rest, and who can never be satiated with human blood. Let us stand on no delicate point of etiquette or diplomatic ceremony. If the proposition is rejected a dozen times, let us tender it again after the next victory ; that the world may be reassured from month to month that we are not responsible for the continuance of this devastation and carnage.

Let it be repeated again and again, to the Northern people, that all we ask, is that they recognize the great principle upon which their own government rests,—*the sovereignty of the States:* and let our own people hold our own government to a strict account for every encroachment upon this vital principle.

Herein lies the simple solution of all these troubles.

If there be any doubt, or any question of doubt, as to the sovereign will of any one of all the States of this Confederacy, or of any border State whose institutions are similar to ours, not in the Confederacy, upon the subject of their present or future alliance, let all armed force be withdrawn ; and let that sovereign will be fairly expressed at the ballot box, by the legal voters of the State ; and let all parties abide by the decision.

Let each State have and freely exercise, the right to determine its own destiny, in its own way. This is all that we have been struggling for from the beginning. It is a principle that secures " rights, inestimable to freemen, and formidable to tyrants only."

Let both governments adopt this mode of settlement, which was bequeathed to them by the great men of the Revolution ; and which has since been adopted by the Emperor Napoleon as the only just mode for the government of States, or even provinces, and the ballot box will soon achieve what the sword cannot accomplish—restore peace to the country; and uphold the great doctrines of State sovereignty and constitutional liberty.

If it is a question of strife, whether Kentucky or Maryland, or any other State, shall cast her lot with the United States, or the Confederate States, there is no mode of settling it so justly, with so little cost, and with so much satisfaction to her own people, as to withdraw all Military force from her limits, and leave the decision, not to the sword, but to the ballot box. If she should decide for herself to abolish slavery and go with the North, the Confederate government can have no just cause of complaint, for that government had its origin in the doctrine that all its just "" powers are derived from the consent of the governed'', and we have no right to insist on governing a sovereign State, against her will. But if she should decide to retain her institutions and go with the South, as we doubt not she will, when the question is fairly submitted to her people at the polls, the Lincoln government must acquiesce, or it must repudiate. and trample upon, the very essential principles on which it was founded, and which were carried out in practice by the fathers of the Republic, for the first half century of its existence.

What Southern man can object to this mode of settlement? It is all that South Carolina, Virginia or Georgia claimed when she seceded from the Union. It is all that either has at any time claimed and all that either ever can justly claim. And what friend of Southern Independence fears the result? What has the Abolition government done to cause the people of any Southern State to desire to reverse her decision and return ingloriously to its embrace? Are we afraid the people of any seceded State, will desire to place the State back in the Abolition union, under the Lincoln despotism, after it has devastated their fields, laid waste their country, burned their cities, slaughtered their sons and degraded their daughters? There is no reason for such fear.

But I may be told that Mr. Lincoln has repudiated this principle in advance, and that it is idle again to tender a settlement upon these terms. This is no reason why we should withhold the repeated renewal of the proposition. Let it be made again and again till the mass of the Northern people understand it; and Mr. Lincoln can not continue to stand before them and the world, stained with the blood of their sons, their husbands and their fathers, and insist, when a proposition so fair is constantly tendered, that thousands of new victims shall still continue to bleed, to gratify his abolition fanaticism, satisfy his revenge, and serve his ambition to govern these States upon the decision of *one tenth* of the people in his favor, against the other *nine tenths*. Let the Northern and Southern mind be brought to contemplate this subject in all its magnitude; and while there may be extreme men on the Northern side, satisfied with nothing less than the subjugation of the South, and the confiscation of our property; and like extremists on the Southern side, whose morbid sensibilities are shocked at the mention of negotiation, or the renewal of an offer by us for a settlement upon any terms; I cannot doubt that the cool-headed thinking men on both sides of the line, who are devoted to the great principles of self government and State sovereignty, including the scar-covered veterans of the army, will finally settle down upon this as the true solution of the great problem which now embarrasses so many millions of people, and will find the higher truth between the two extremes.

If, upon the sober second thought, the public sentiment North sustains the policy of Mr. Lincoln, when he proposes by the power of the sword to place the great doctrines of the Declaration of Independence and the Constitution of his country under his feet, and proclaims his purpose to govern these States by military power, when he shall have obtained the consent of *one tenth* of the governed; how can

42

the same public sentiment condemn him, if, at the head of his vast armies he shall proclaim himself Emperor of the whole country ; and submit the question to the vote of the Northern people, and when he has obtained, as he could easily do, the vote of *one tenth* in his favor, he shall insist on his right to govern them as their legitimate sovereign? If he is right in principle in the one case, he would unquestionably be right in the other. If he may rightfully continue the war against the South to sustain the one, why may he not as rightfully turn his armies against the North to establish the other?

But the timid among us may say, how are we to meet and repel his armies, if Mr. Lincoln shall continue to reject these terms, and shall be sustained by the sentiment of the North? as he claims not only the right to govern us, but he claims the right to take from us all that we have.

The answer is plain. Let every man do his duty ; and let us as a people place our trust in God, and we shall certainly repel his assaults, and achieve our Independence ; and if true to ourselves and to posterity, we shall maintain our Constitutional liberty also. The achievement of our Independence is a great object : but not greater than the preservation of Constitutional liberty.

The good man cannot read the late proclamation of Mr. Lincoln, without being struck with the resemblance between it, and a similar one, issued several thousand years ago, by Ben-hadad, king of Syria. That wicked king, denied in others the right of self-government ; and vaunting himself in numbers, and putting his trust in chariots and horses, he invaded Israel, and beseiged Samaria with an overwhelming force. When the king of Israel, with a small band, resisted his entrance into the city, the Syrian king sent him this message : " Thou shalt deliver me thy silver and thy gold, and thy wives, and thy children ; yet I will send my servants unto thee to-morrow, about this time ; and they shall search thy house, and the houses of thy servants ; and it shall be, that whatsoever is pleasant in thine eyes, they shall put in their hands and take it away." The king of Israel consulted the Elders, after receiving this arrogant message, and replied : " This thing I may not do." Ben-hadad, enraged at this reply, and confident of his strength, sent back and said :

"The Gods do so to me, and more also, if the dust of Samaria shall suffice, for handfuls, for all the people that follow me." The king of Israel answered and said : "Tell him, let not him that girdeth on his harness, boast himself as he that putteth it off."

The result was, that the small band of Israelites guided by Jehovah, attacked the Syrian armies and routed them with great slaughter, and upon a second trial of strength, the Syrian armies were destroyed and their king made captive.

When Mr. Lincoln, following the example of this wicked king, and relying upon his chariots, and his horsemen, and his vast armies, to sustain a cause equally unjust. proclaims to us, that *all we have is his,* and that he will send his servants, whose numbers are overwhelming, with arms in their hands to take it, and threatens vengeance if we resist, let us—" Tell him, let not him that girdeth on his harness boast himself as he that putteth it off." "The race is not to the swift, nor the battle to the strong." " God is the judge, he putteth down one and setteth up another."

Not doubting the justice of our cause, let us stand in our allotted places; and in the name of Him who rules the hosts of Heaven, and the armies of Earth, let us contiue to strike for liberty and independence, and our efforts will ultimately be crowned with triumphant success.

JOSEPH E. BROWN.

APPENDIX.

ACT OF SIXTEENTH CHARLES I, CHAPTER 10.

THIS WENT INTO OPERATION 1ST AUGUST, 1641.

An Act for the regulating of the privy council, and for taking away the Court commonly called the Star-Chamber.

WHEREAS by the Great Charter *many times confirmed in parliament,* it is enacted, That *no freeman shall be taken or imprisoned, or disseized of his freehold or liberties, or free customs, or be outlawed, or exiled, or otherwise destroyed ; and that the King will not pass upon him, or condemn him, but by lawful judgment of his peers, or by the law of the land.*

(2.) And by another statute made in the fifth year of the reign of King Edward, it is enacted, that no man shall be *attached by any accusation, nor forejudged of life, or limb,* nor his *lands, tenements, goods* nor *chattels seized into the King's hands, against the form of the* GREAT CHARTER and the LAW OF THE LAND ;

(3.) And by another statute made in the five and twentieth year of the reign of the same King Edward the Third, it is accorded, assented, and established, that *none shall be taken by petition, or suggestion made to the King, or to his council,* unless it be by *indictment* er *presentment* of *good* and *lawful people of the same neighborhood,* where such deeds be done, in due manner, or by process made by *writ original* at the *common law ;* and that *none be put out of his franchise, or freehold,* unless he be *duly* brought in to answer, and forejudged of the same *by the course of the law :* And if anything be done against the same, it shall be *redressed,* and *holden for none.* (4) And by another statute made in the eight and twentieth year of the reign of the same King Edward the Third, it is, amongst other things, enacted, That *no man*, of what estate or condition soever he be, *shall be put out of his lands and tenements, nor taken, nor imprisoned, nor disinherited, without being brought in to answer by* DUE PROCESS of LAW. (5) And by another statute made in the two and fortieth year of the reign of the said King Edward the Third, it is enacted, That *no man* be put to answer without *presentment* before justices or *matter* of record, or by *due process* and *writ original,* according to the OLD LAW *of the land :* And if anything be done to the contrary, it shall be *void in law* and *holden for error.* (6) And by another statute in the six and thirtieth year of the reign of the same King Edward the Third, it is, amongst other things, Enacted, That all pleas, which shall be pleaded in any courts, before any of the King's justices, or in his other places or before any of his other ministers, or in the courts and places of any other lords within this realm, shall be entered and enrolled in Latin. (7) And whereas by the statute made in the third year of King Henry the Seventh, power is given to the Chancellor, the lord treasurer of England, for the time being, and the keeper of the King's Privy seal, or two of them, calling unto them a bishop, and a temporal lord of the King's most honorable council, and the two chief justices of the King's bench, and common pleas for the time being, or other two justices in their absence, to proceed as in that act is expressed, for the punishment of some particular offences therein mentioned. (8) And by the statute made in the one and twentieth year of King Henry the Eighth, the president of the council associated to join with the lord chancellor, and other judges in the said statute of the third of Henry the Seventh mentioned. (9) But the said judges have not kept themselves to the points limited by the said statute, but have undertaken to punish where *no law doth warrant,* and to make decrees for things, having *no such authority,* and to inflict heavier punishments, *than by any law is warranted.*

2. And forasmuch as all matters examinable or determinable before the said judges or in the court commonly called the *star-chamber,* may have their proper remedy and redress, and their due punishment and correction by the *common law of the land,* and in the *ordinary course of justice* elsewhere. (2) And forasmuch as the reasons and motives, inducing the erection and continuance of that court do now cease. (3) And the proceedings, censures, and decrees of that court, have by experience been found to be an intolerable burthen to the subject, and the means to introduce *an arbitrary power and government.* (4) And for as much as the council table hath of late times assumed unto itself, a power to intermeddle in civil and matters only of private interest between party and party; and have ADVENTURED to determine of the *estates* and *liberties of the subjects, contrary to the* LAWS *of*

the LAND, *and the* Rights *and* Privileges *of the subject,* by which great and manifold mischiefs and inconveniences have arisen and happened, and much incertainty, by means of such proceedings, hath been conceived concerning men's rights and estates; for settling whereof and Preventing the like in time to come,

3. Be it ordained and Enacted *by the authority of this present parliament,* That the said court commonly called the star-chamber, and all jurisdictions, power and authority, belonging unto, or exercised in the same court, or by any the judges, officers, or ministers thereof, be from the first day of August, in the year of our Lord God one thousand six hundred forty and one, CLEARLY *and* ABSOLUTELY *dissolved, taken away, and determined.* (2) And that from the said first day of August, neither the lord chancellor or keeper of the Great seal of England, the lord treasurer of England, the keeper of the King's Privy seal, or president of the council, nor any bishop, temporal lord, privy counsellor or judge, or justice whatsoever, shall have any power or authority to hear, examine or determine any matter or thing whatsoever, in the said court, commonly called the Star-Chamber, or to make, pronounce, or deliver any judgment, sentence, order or decree; or to do any judicial or ministerial act in the said court. (3) And that all and every act and acts of parliament, and all and every article, clause, and sentence in them, and every of them, by which any jurisdiction, power or authority is given, limited or appointed unto the said court, commonly called the Star-Chamber, or unto all, or any of the judges, officers, or ministers thereof, or for any proceedings to be had or made in the said court, or for any matter or thing to be drawn into question, examined or determined there, shall for so much as concerneth the said court of Star-Chamber, and the power and authority thereby given unto it, be from the *first* day of *August* REPEALED and ABSOLUTELY REVOKED and *made void.*

4. And be it likewise Enacted, That the like jurisdiction now used and exercised in the court, before the president and council in the marches of Wales; (2) And also in the court, before the president and council established in the northern ports; (3) And also in the court commonly called the court of the duchy of Lancaster, held before the chancellor and council of that court; (4) And also in the court of Exchequer of the *county palatine of Chester,* held before the chamberlain and council of that court; (5) The like jurisdiction being exercised there, shall, from the said *first* day of *August one thousand six hundred forty-one,* be also REPEALED, and ABSOLUTELY REVOKED, and *made* VOID; *any law, prescription, custom or usage, or the said statute made in the third year of King* Henry the Seventh, *or the*

statute made in the one and twentieth of Henry the Eighth, *or any act or acts of parliament heretofore had or made, to the contrary thereof, in any wise notwithstanding.* (6) AND THAT FROM HENCEFORTH NO court, council or PLACE OF JUDICATURE, SHALL BE ERECTED, ORDAINED, CONSTITUTED OR APPOINTED WITHIN THIS REALM OF *England*, OR DOMINION OF *Wales*, WHICH SHALL HAVE, USE, OR EXERCISE THE SAME, OR THE LIKE JURISDICTION, AS IS OR HATH BEEN USED, PRACTICED OR EXERCISED IN THE SAID COURT OF *Star-Chamber.*

5. Be it likewise declared, and Enacted by the authority of this present parliament, That *neither his* MAJESTY, NOR *his* PRIVY COUNCIL, HAVE, or OUGHT TO HAVE *any jurisdiction, power or authority, by English bill, petition, articles, libels, or any other* ARBITRARY WAY WHATSOEVER, *to examine or draw into question, determine or dispose of the lands, tenements, hereditaments, goods or chattels of any of the subjects of this kingdom ; but that the same ought to be tried, and determined in the ordinary courts of justice and by the ordinary course of law.*

6. And be it further provided and enacted, that if any lord chancellor or keeper of the Great seal of England ; lord treasurer, keeper of the king's privy seal, president of the council, bishop, temporal lord, privy counsellor, judge or justice *whatsoever,* shall offend, or do anything contrary to the purport, true intent, and meaning of this law, then he or they for such offence *forfeit* the sum FIVE HUNDRED POUNDS of lawful money of England, unto any party grieved, his executors or administrators, who shall really prosecute for the same, and first obtain judgment thereupon to be recovered in any Court of record at *Westminister,* by action of debt, bill, plaint, or information, wherein no essoign, protection, wager of law, aid prayer, *privilege,* injunction or order of restraint, *shall be* IN ANY WISE *prayed, granted or allowed,* nor any more than one imparlance. (2) And if any person, against whom, any such judgment or recovery shall be had as aforesaid, shall, after such judgment or recovery, *offend again,* in the same, then he or they for such offence shall forfeit the sum of ONE THOUSAND POUNDS of lawful money of England, unto any party grieved, his executors or administrators, who shall really prosecute for the same, and first obtain judgment thereupon, to be recovered in any court of record at *Westminister.* by action of debt, bill, plaint, or information, inwhich no essoign, protection. wager of law, aid prayer, *privilege,* injunction or order of restraint, shall be IN ANY WISE *prayed, granted or allowed ;* nor any more than one imparlance. (3) And if any person, against whom any such second judgment or recovery shall be had as aforesaid, shall after such judgment of recovery *offend again* in the same kind, and shall be thereof duly convicted by in-

dictment, information, or any other lawful way or means, that such person so convicted shall be from thenceforth DISABLED, and become, by virtue of this act INCAPA-BLE, *ipso facto, to bear his and their said office and offices respectively.* (4) And shall be likewise *disabled to make any gift, grant, conveyance, or other disposition, of any of his lands, tenements, hereditaments, goods or chattels ; or to make any benefit of any gifts,* conveyance. or legacy, to his own use.

7. And *every person so offending.* shall likewise forfeit and loose *to the party grieved,* by anything done. contrary to the true intent and meaning of this law, his *trible damages,* which he shall sustain and be put unto, by means or occasion of any such act, or thing done ; the same to be recovered in any of his Majesty's courts of record at Westminister, by action of debt, bill, plaint, or information, wherein no essoign, protection, wager of law, aid prayer, *privilege,* injunction, or order of restraint, *shall be* IN ANY WISE *prayed, granted or allowed,* nor any more than one imparlance.

8. And be it also provided and enacted, That if any person shall hereafter be committed, restrained of his liberty, or suffer imprisonment, by the order or decree of any such court of STAR-CHAMBER, or other court aforesaid, now, or at any time hereafter, having, or pretending to have, the same, or like jurisdiction, power or authority, to *commit* or *imprison* as aforesaid ; (2) Or by the command or warrant of the *king's Majesty, his heirs and successors in their own person ;* or by the command or warrant of the *council-board ; or of any of the lords,* or *others of his Majesty's privy council ;* (3) That in every such case, every person so *committed, restrained* of his liberty, or *suffering imprisonment,* upon demands or motion made by his counsel, or other employed by him for that purpose, unto the Judges of the court of king's bench, or common pleas, in open court, shall, without delay, upon any pretence whatsoever. for the ordinary fees usually paid for the same, have forthwith granted unto him a writ of *habeas corpus,* to be directed generally unto all and every sheriff, gaoler, minister, officer, or other person, in whose custody the person committed or restrained, shall be. (4) And the sheriffs, gaoler, minister. officer, or other person, in whose custody the person so committed or restrained shall be, shall, at the return of the said writ and according to the command thereof, upon due and convenient notice thereof, given unto him, at the charge of the party who requireth or prosecuteth such writ, and upon security by his *own bond* given, to pay the charge of carrying back the prisoner, if he shall be remanded by the court to which he shall be brought ; as in like cases hath been used ; such charges of bringing up, and carrying back the prisoner, to be always ordered by the court, if any difference shall arise thereabout ; bring or cause to be brought, the body of the said party so committed or restrained, unto and before the Judges or justices of the said court,

from whence the same writ shall issue, in open court. (5 And shall then likewise certify the *true cause* of such, his *detainer*, or imprisonment, and thereupon the court, within three court days after such return, made and delivered in open court, shall proceed to *examine* and *determine*, whether the cause of such commitment, appearing upon the said return, be just and legal or not, and shall thereupon do what to JUSTICE SHALL APPERTAIN, either by *delivering, bailing*, or *remanding* the prisoner. (6) And if anything shall be otherwise wilfully done, or omitted to be done by any judge, justice, officer or other person afore-mentioned, contrary to the directions and true meaning hereof, then such persons so offending shall forfeit to *the party grieved, his treble damages* to be recovered by such means, and in such manner as is formerly in this act, limited and appointed, for the like penalty to be sued for and recovered.

9. Provided always, and be it enacted, That this act and the several clauses therein contained shall be taken and expounded to extend only to the court of STAR-CHAMBER: (2) And to the said court holden before the *president* and *council* in the *marches* of Wales; (3) And before the *president* and *council* in the *Northern parts*; (4) And also to the court commonly called the *court of the* duchy of Lancaster holden before the *chancellor* and *council* of that court: (5) And also, in the court of Exchequer, of the *county palatine* of Chester, held before the *chamberlain* and *council* of that court; (6) And to *all courts of like jurisdiction to be hereafter* erected, ordained, constituted, or appointed, as aforesaid; and to the warrants and directions of the *council-board*, and to the *commitments, restraints* and *imprisonments* of any person or persons, made, commanded or awarded by the *king's Majesty, his heirs or successors, in their own person,* or by the *lords,* and *others of the privy council, and every one of them.*

And lastly, provided and be it enacted, That no person or persons shall be sued, impleaded, molested or troubled, for any offence against this present act, unless the party supposed to have so offended, shall be, sued, or impleaded for the same, within *two years,* at the most, after such time, wherein the said offence shall be committed.

www.ingramcontent.com/pod-product-compliance
Lightning Source LLC
Chambersburg PA
CBHW030906260626
47169CB00008B/2712